This edition published by Kids Can Press in 2021

Originally published under the title *Can You See Me? A Book About Being Tiny*.
Text and illustrations © 2020 Gökçe İrten

Translation rights arranged through the VeroK Agency, Barcelona, Spain
North American English edition © 2021 Kids Can Press

Published in Canada and the U.S. by Kids Can Press Ltd.
25 Dockside Drive, Toronto, ON M5A 0B5

Kids Can Press is a Corus Entertainment Inc. company

www.kidscanpress.com

The artwork in this book was created using mixed media and Photoshop.
The text is hand-lettered.

Printed and bound in Buji, Shenzhen, China, in 3/2021 by WKT Company

MIX
Paper from
responsible sources
FSC® C010256
www.fsc.org

CM 21 0 9 8 7 6 5 4 3 2 1

Library and Archives Canada Cataloguing in Publication

Title: Can you see me? : a book about feeling small / Gökçe İrten.
Names: İrten, Gökçe, author, illustrator.
Identifiers: Canadiana 20210127457 | ISBN 9781525308376 (hardcover)
Subjects: LCSH: Size perception — Juvenile literature. | LCSH: Size judgment —
Juvenile literature. | LCSH: Attitude (Psychology) — Juvenile literature.
Classification: LCC BF299.S5 C36 2021 | DDC j153.7/52 — dc23

Kids Can Press gratefully acknowledges that the land on which our office is
located is the traditional territory of many nations, including the Mississaugas of
the Credit, the Anishnabeg, the Chippewa, the Haudenosaunee and the Wendat
peoples, and is now home to many diverse First Nations, Inuit and Métis peoples.

We thank the Government of Ontario, through Ontario Creates, for supporting
our publishing activity.

To my lovely family ♡

A Book About Feeling Small

CAN YOU SEE ME?

GÖKÇE İRTEN

KIDS CAN PRESS

Can you see him?
You have to look REALLY closely.

Some things around us are <u>small</u>,
and some things around us are <u>big</u>.
Buildings, planes, streets and cities are big.
Paper clips, daisies, pencil sharpeners
and teaspoons are small.
But are they really?

It can depend on where you're standing.
Take, for example, an airplane.
It looks huge when you're beside it,
    but it looks tiny in the sky.

Do you sometimes feel small?

Let's think some more.
An orangutan is about the same size
as a human (though a bit stronger
and definitely more orange).

Everything around you would seem
very different if you were as
small as him.

I mean him. $\longrightarrow$

If you zoomed in 100 times while taking a photo of an itchy orangutan, you might see a flea jumping in an orange forest.

And if you could jump as high as a flea,
you wouldn't have to climb the 1665 steps to
get to the top of the Eiffel Tower if the elevator broke.

NOTE: Some fleas
can jump up to 100
times their own height.
But they are so tiny
you have to look
really carefully to
see it happen.

you

324 meters
(1063 feet)

An ant can carry 50 times its own weight.
If an ant were as big as you,
it would be like you carrying a rhinoceros.

But it looks like this
when it carries a tiny leaf.

Tiny?!

← ant

you

If your foot could grow as fast as
a caterpillar can during its life cycle ...

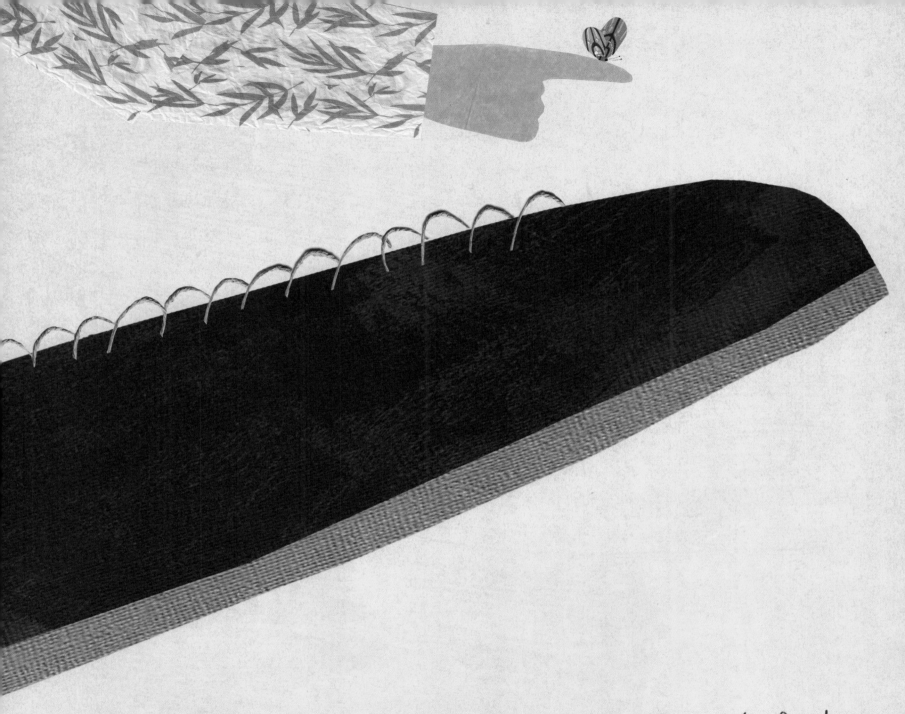

...your foot would be 3 times larger after just a few days.

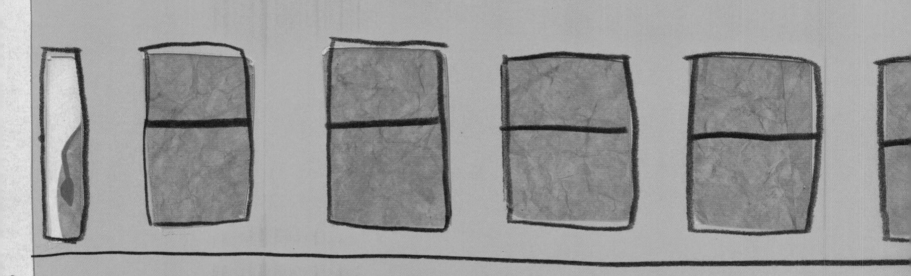

SCHOOL BUS

It would keep growing until it was so big
it would not fit in a school bus.
Like this elephant.

FINISH

Ladybugs can float in water
for 24 hours.
If you could float like
a ladybug, you could become
a champion floater ...

...but you'd need a bigger pool.

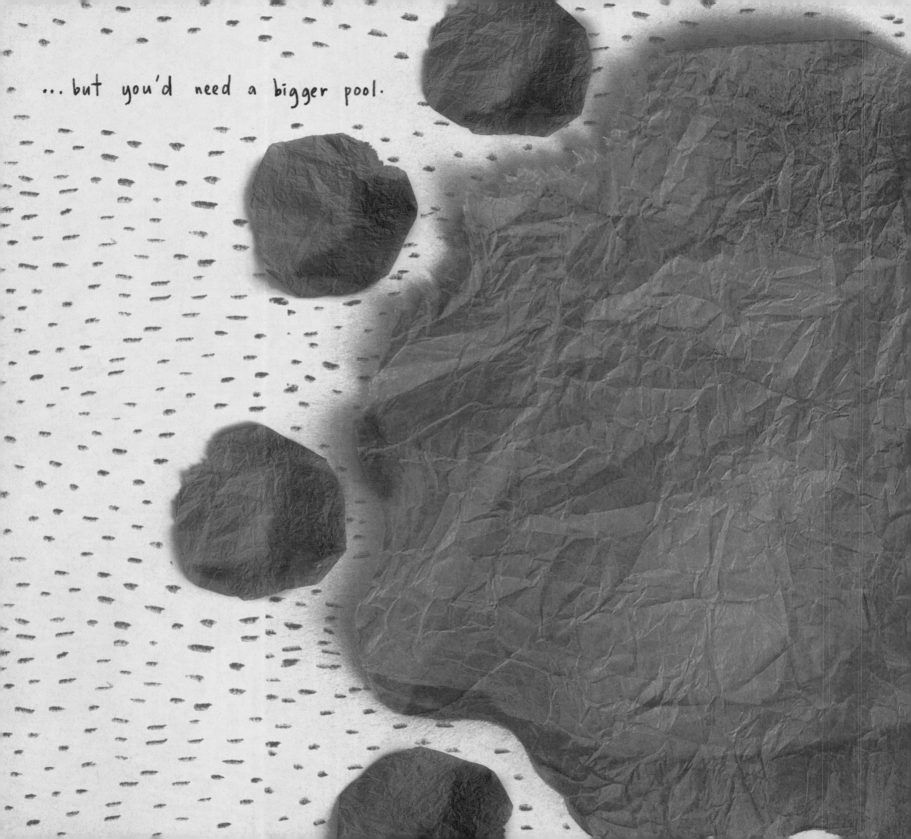

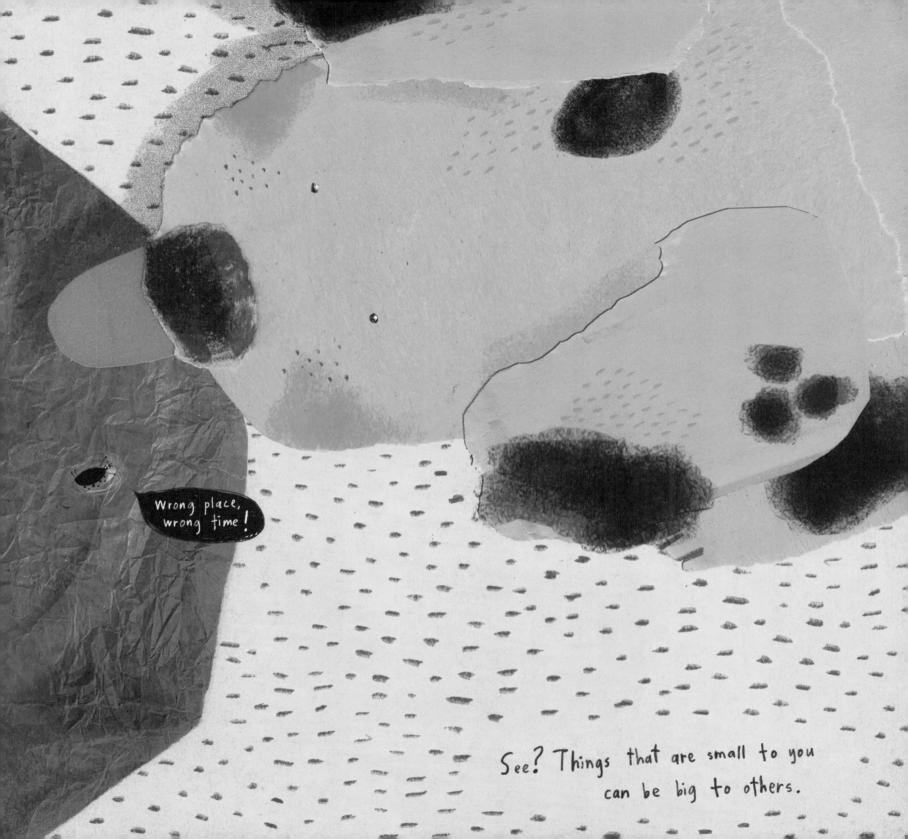

Elephants are so big that when one of
their footprints fills with water,
it creates a natural habitat
for more than 60 different species.

Whether you feel small or big
depends on who you are.
A chicken must look so scary to an ant!

But to others, ants might look like giants.

Can you imagine being so small that this triangle looks like the Great Pyramid?

If you were a small insect,
what would sightseeing be like?

In a miniature world,
almost anything can become a home ...

... or a vehicle.

Things that are small to you ...

... are like countries,
or even planets, to others.

We live in a big world
with many small worlds in it.